LITTLE HOUSE

Laura Ingalls Wilder

MY FIRST LITTLE HOUSE BOOKS

A

LITTLE PRAIRIE HOUSE

ADAPTED FROM THE LITTLE HOUSE BOOKS

By Laura Ingalls Wilder

Illustrated by Renée Graef

HARPERCOLLINS PUBLISHERS

For Marce
—R.G.

A Little Prairie House   Text adapted from Little House on the Prairie, copyright 1935, 1963 Little House Heritage Trust.   Illustrations copyright © 1998 by Renée Graef.
Manufactured in China. All rights reserved.   Library of Congress Cataloging-in-Publication Data   A little prairie house : adapted from the Little house books by Laura Ingalls
Wilder / illustrated by Renée Graef.   p.   cm. — (My first Little house books)   Text adapted from Little house on the prairie.   Summary: A family travels to a new home
on the prairie, where they build a house and meet a friendly neighbor.   ISBN 0-06-025907-8. — ISBN 0-06-025908-6 (lib. bdg.) — ISBN 0-06-443526-1 (pbk.)   1. Wilder,
Laura Ingalls, 1867-1957—Juvenile Fiction.   [1. Wilder, Laura Ingalls, 1867-1957—Fiction.   2. Frontier and pioneer life—Great Plains—Fiction.   3. Family life—
Great Plains—Fiction.   4. Great Plains—Fiction.]   I. Wilder, Laura Ingalls, 1867-1957. Little house on the prairie.   II. Graef, Renée, ill.   III. Series.   PZ7.L7352
1998   96-24060   [E]—DC20   CIP   AC   ❖   HarperCollins®, 🏰®, and Little House® are trademarks of HarperCollins Publishers Inc.   www.littlehousebooks.com
Weekly Reader is a registered trademark of the Weekly Reader Corporation. 2003 Edition

Illustrations for the My First Little House Books are inspired by the work of Garth Williams with his permission, which we gratefully acknowledge.

Once upon a time, a little girl named Laura traveled in a covered wagon across the giant prairie. She traveled with her Pa, her Ma, her big sister Mary, her little sister Carrie, and their good old bulldog Jack. They were searching for the perfect place to build themselves a little house.

One day, after the little family had been traveling across the prairie for a long time, Laura and Mary woke up earlier than the sun. They ate their breakfast of cornmeal mush and hurried to help Ma wash the dishes. Pa was loading everything into the wagon.

When the sun rose, they were driving across the prairie. There was no road to drive on, so Pet and Patty, the two gentle mustangs, waded through the grasses.

Later that morning, Pa said, "Whoa!" The wagon stopped. "Here we are!" he said. "Right here we'll build our house."

Laura and Mary jumped to the ground. All around them there was nothing but prairie.

Right away, Pa and Ma began to unload the wagon. They took everything out and piled it on the ground while Laura and Mary and Jack watched. Then Pa drove the wagon down into the prairie, out of sight, to get a load of logs from the creek bottom.

Laura was a little frightened to be left on the prairie without the wagon. She wanted to hide in the tall grass like a little prairie chicken. But instead she helped Ma, while Mary sat on the grass and minded Baby Carrie.

Soon Pa came back with a load of logs. For days
and days Pa kept hauling logs. He made two piles
of them, one for the house and one for the stable.
When he had enough logs, it was time to build.
Pa began the house first.

All by himself, Pa built the walls of the house three logs high, and then Ma helped him. Log by log, Pa and Ma built the walls higher and higher. Soon Laura couldn't climb over them any more.

Then one day Pa was off hunting, and he came home whistling merrily. "Good news!" he shouted. Pa had met a neighbor on the other side of the creek. His name was Mr. Edwards, and he was going to help Pa finish building the house. Then Pa would help Mr. Edwards build his house.

Early the next morning, Mr. Edwards came. He was lean and tall, and he bowed to Ma politely. He told Laura he was a wildcat from Tennessee, and he could spit farther than Laura had ever imagined anyone could spit. Laura tried and tried, but she could never spit so far or so well as Mr. Edwards could.

Mr. Edwards was a fast worker. In one day he and Pa built the walls of the little house as high as Pa wanted them. They sang while they worked, and their axes made the chips fly. They cut a tall hole for the door, and square holes for the windows.

Laura couldn't wait to see the inside of the house, and as soon as the tall hole was cut, she ran inside. Stripes of sunshine came through the cracks in the walls and went all across Laura's hands and arms and feet.

At the end of the day, Mr. Edwards said he would go home, but Pa and Ma said he must stay to supper. Ma had made stewed jackrabbit and steaming-hot, thick cornbread with molasses. Mr. Edwards said he surely did appreciate that supper. Then Pa took out his fiddle and began to sing.

Suddenly Mr. Edwards jumped up and began to dance.
He danced like a jumping-jack in the moonlight,
while Pa's fiddle kept on rollicking, and Laura's and
Mary's hands were clapping together. Pa played and
played, and Mr. Edwards danced and danced.

Finally Mr. Edwards said he must go. "Play me down the road!" he said. So Pa played, and Pa and Laura and Mr. Edwards sang with all their might until Laura could not hear Mr. Edwards any more. Only the wind rustled in the prairie grasses, and the big yellow moon sailed high over the new little house on the prairie.